Sourdough Scott's Bedtime Fairy Tales From Alaska

Daniel S. Janik

Illustrated by Patricia A. Kilson
Foreword by Ted Ireton

Since 1978

PO Box 221974 Anchorage,, Alaska 99522-1974

ISBN 978-1-59433-031-5

Library of Congress Catalog Card Number: 2005908075

Manufactured in the United States of America.

Dedication

To readers of all ages everywhere, who, in
their hearts, are children of the Far North—
from their forever friend, Sourdough Scott.

Foreword

I am an Alaska Eskimo and have known Sourdough Scott for over 40 years. There is simply no finer friend in all the land.

As kids, we explored the Land of the Midnight Sun together. We skied in the snow, panned for gold, and then turned right around and fished the same streams for salmon, grayling, and Dolly Varden. Some of our best times together were hiking the mountains looking for blueberries to eat and put away for blueberry pies. I remember eating them 'til our tongues turned blue! Together, we shared the joy of seeing wild moose, Dall sheep, and grizzly bears playing in the Great Land.

Most people know that Alaska is big, beautiful, and cold in winter. But those of us who have lived in the

Far North, know that one of its most important attributes is the warm hearts of its people. If these tales awaken in you more than wonder — maybe a sort of awe — about Alaska and its Native culture, then I invite you to find out more about its people.

I remember being around many a warm camp fire with Sourdough Scott hearing and telling stories together — stories that kept me entranced and excited. These three stories are some of Sourdough Scott's best and I hope he writes many, many more for you and me to enjoy.

Ted Ireton,
Best friend of Sourdough Scott

Tale 1
Three Bears

In a small Eskimo village in Alaska, so far North and West that no trees or bushes would grow and no mountains dared peek their heads above the flat, squishy tundra, which extended in every direction as far as the eye could see, lived an old Eskimo man, his wife, and their three sons.

Now, all three sons were exactly the same age, but each was very different in the way he looked and acted, and as you may well guess, this was a source of never-ending talk among the village people.

The first son was almost as big as a caribou. He was, however, rather shy and kept mostly to himself. His name was Atlak, which means different one, for he had coarse, white hair which he let grow down to his shoulders.

Atlak liked swimming in the cold, arctic water. In spite of his unusualness, he was a very loyal son.

The second was not as big as the first, but still, he was as big as any man in the village, and maybe even a bit bigger than most. He was known everywhere for his great strength and ill temper. His name was Aivik, which means walrus, for he was as strong as a walrus. He had bristly brown hair which he wore quite long and shaggy, but not as long as his brothers. In spite of his appearance, he was a very loyal son.

The third son was smaller than either of his two brothers, but he was swift and agile. He was known mostly for his curiosity and love of exploring. His name was Akpik, which means salmonberry, for he loved berries. He had short, coarse, black hair and was also a very loyal son.

One day the three sons were walking together along a reindeer path, arguing as brothers will about various things of no consequence, when suddenly they stopped in their tracks and stared. There, standing by a great wood and mud house, or *innui*, was the most beautiful girl any of them had ever seen, and all three fell in love with her instantly. It soon became apparent to each of the brothers that the others desired her too.

Eventually, a great argument broke out between them, which could easily have led to a mean fight. However, as I said before, the brothers were loyal brothers, so they decided to take the problem to their father, and vowed among themselves that they would abide by whatever his decision might be.

When they returned home and explained the situation to their father, he became quiet and very sad, for you see, he loved all his sons equally and could not decide among them. It was their mother who finally broke the silence and said, "I have a solution. The girl you all pine for is the daughter of the most powerful shaman, or medicine man, in all the world. He will be wise enough to figure out what to do."

This seemed a sensible solution to the father, who didn't want to lose his sons' love, and his sons being the loyal sons they were, agreed to do whatever was his wish in this matter. So the father sent his wife to the innui of the most powerful shaman in the world to ask for his daughter and also to decide which of his three sons should have her.

The wife, knowing that the shaman loved his daughter dearly, did not try to bargain with him for her. Instead, she picked out her finest fur parka, or coat, her finest mukluks, or boots, and three of the strongest husky-dogs they had, all good sled dogs who knew gee, or right, from haw, or left, and gave them directly to the shaman.

Now, as you can imagine, the shaman was very pleased with the gifts, but even then was still not excited about losing his daughter. So, wise man that he was, he said to the wife, "Your gifts are as generous as your family is great. I will therefore accept them and grant your petition that my daughter marry one of your sons. However, since my daughter is also great and is deserving of the best, and because I cannot decide which of your sons is the best, I would instead give them all a task, and the first one to complete this task, within one year, and return to me will have her. But all three must agree that if none completes the task in the allotted time, all must serve me as if they were my loyal sons 'til the end of my days." By this he hoped to keep the gifts and his daughter, and to gain three sons to help him in his old age.

So the wife left the gifts and quickly returned home to her husband and told him faithfully all that had been said.

Now while the father's heart grieved for his sons' desires, he knew the shaman to be a crafty man, and that it would not go well for his sons if they agreed to such folly, so he decided to tell them nothing. But the sons kept asking him day in and day out about nothing except the girl they all loved, until at last he could stand it no more and told them the whole story. He begged them over and over not to accept this challenge, but since the sons' eyes were totally blinded by their love, they all three went directly to the shaman and quickly agreed to his terms.

So, that evening, the shaman prepared a great feast for the brothers, in their honor, for he felt they deserved this if they were willing to risk everything for his daughter. And after the feast, he had them assemble about him and his daughter before a great fire and told them their task. "You must each go your way and whoever returns here first with a hundred names for snow shall have my daughter. But beware, for if none of you completes the task within one year of this day, you must all serve me as if you were my own loyal sons 'til the end of my days."

After several moments of
silence,
the
brothers
all agreed,
and they im-
mediately set
off in different
directions to dis-
cover the hun-
dred names for
snow.

Now this task may sound very strange to you, but to
the Eskimo there are many different kinds of snow:
wet snow, dry snow, crunchy snow, icy snow, and on
and on. And any person who knows a hundred names
for snow would have to be smart, and would probably be a good provider for his daughter even in the
worst of winters. This the shaman knew. Still, even
he did not know a hundred names for snow.

The year passed slowly and finally the day
came when the brothers had to return.
And when they all returned, the shaman
again prepared a feast for the brothers
in their honor, for he felt they deserved
this, since they had all returned as they had
promised so long ago.

And, after the feast, he had them assemble about
him and his daughter, who seemed to have grown
even more beautiful during the year, if that is
possible. He asked the first son, Atlak, the biggest and most different, quiet and retiring, Atlak
of the long white hair, who was indeed a loyal son,
"What are the hundred names of snow?"

Though Atlak had had many
daring adventures, and seen
many wondrous things
in his long journey,
he could recite
only forty-nine
names for
snow and so
hung his
head in
sorrow.

The shaman then turned to the second son, Aivik, the strongest, the ill-tempered, Aivik of the bristly brown hair who was also a loyal son. "What are the hundred names of snow?"

And though Aivik recounted many exciting events, and had seen many interesting things in his long searches, he could name only fifty-nine names for snow and so hung his head in sorrow alongside his first brother.

At last, the shaman turned to the third and last son, Akpik, the smallest, swiftest and most agile, Akpik of the coarse black hair who was also a loyal son, "What are the hundred names of snow?"

Now Akpik, being very curious and adventurous, had had many intriguing experiences in his long sojourn, and he quickly named forty-nine names of snow, then fifty-nine, then sixty-nine and so on 'til at last he came to the ninety-ninth name. But try as he might, he could not think of a hundredth name for snow. Finally, after considerable trying, and the best of coaching from his brothers and the best of encouragement from the shaman, who really thought he should succeed given how close he was to completing the task, and, of course, with the strongest of encouragement from his daughter, who really loved Akpik the best of all—he hung his head in sorrow and joined his brothers.

Now this was very disappointing to the shaman, who had come to quite like all the brothers and who had just decided that any young man who was a loyal son, loved his daughter enough to take on any task for her, and then, even when he knew he would fail the task, returned as he had promised to live by his word, was really deserving of his daughter and just the kind of person he would like for a son-in-law.

But in spite of his feelings, each of the brothers swore before him that since they could not have his daughter, as they had agreed, they would each serve the shaman the rest of his life, and in addition, so great was their sadness that they agreed that none of them would have the woman they so desired.

But while the shaman turned his back to tell his daughter the sad news, the brothers fell to quarreling, then to fighting, and finally were about to kill each other in their anguish.

The shaman, seeing this, and knowing that once made, an oath must not be broken, quickly summoned all his great power and turned the brothers each into bears, and they ran out of the great innui, each in different directions: Atlak, the biggest, the quiet and retiring Atlak of the long white hair who so dearly loved the water, fled to the Far North to the great ice floes and eventually became the father of all polar bears.

Aivik, the strong and ill-tempered, Aivik of the bristly brown hair, fled to the hills of the Interior and eventually became the father of all grizzly bears, including the greatest of them all, the Kodiak bears.

And Akpik, the smallest, swiftest, most agile, Akpik of the coarse black hair, who loved berries so dearly, ran off to the deep alder forests and eventually became the father of all black bears.

And now you know why bears are all brothers, and yet are so different in the way they look and act, and how they came to be.

Tale 2
Wolf and Moon

Once upon a time, in a land so far north that, in fact, there was no land at all but only ice and constant snow, there lived a handsome young Eskimo and a beautiful maiden. They had been friends for almost as long as they could remember, and had grown to love each other very much over the years. However, each was somewhat selfish, and it was not long before they found that in spite of their love, they could not get along well together.

Whenever the young man wanted to talk to the maiden, she would busy herself with things that needed to be done. And whenever the maiden wanted the young man's attentions, he would always find something that had yet to be done. So their times together were difficult, as you may guess.

One especially dark winter night, they decided to put on their fur parkas, or coats, and their fur mukluks, or boots, and hike through the snow to visit a friend.

Now this friend was not an ordinary friend. He was an old man who, it was said, was once a powerful shaman, or magician. However, these days, most of the young people thought of him as just a crazy old man, and generally left him alone. The young man and maiden, on the other hand, took pity on him, and visited him every so often bringing him news from the village. You see, in spite of their problems, the young man and maiden were really very kind at heart.

So together, mitten in mitten, the young man and maiden trudged through the snow and storm until at last they reached the old man's igloo, or ice house, and knocked on an ice block at its entrance.
"Who dares disturb the great shaman? Be gone and quickly!" came a deep foreboding voice from within as if the igloo itself could speak.

"It is your friends from the village," said the young man.

"We've come to visit with you awhile," said the maiden.

All of a sudden, warmth and cheerful light burst from within the igloo to greet them. As they crawled in, brushed the loose snow from their parkas, took off their mukluks, and entered the large room, it seemed as if the cold, dark, and storm were suddenly whisked miles away! And that was odd, you see because, although the young man and maiden checked all around the entrance, they could see no door to shut out the cold!

After a few moments of silence, it seemed as though the igloo itself spoke and said, "You know, it is not polite to stare!" And as suddenly as this was spoken, an old man appeared from behind them, smiling mischievously.

"Hrumpf! Got some work to do on that entrance enchantment, I can see. I made it strong to keep out the storm, but it seems to have developed some bad manners. But enough of that! Welcome, my young friends. Sit down here by my seal oil-lamp and warm yourselves. Tell me the news and what it is you wish of me."

As you can see, shaman or not, the old man was very perceptive about people. And, after all, the man and maiden were really two of his best friends.

The young man and maiden sat down by the oil-lamp and its meager flame suddenly sputtered.

"Humpf! Must have put too much eagerness in the oil-lamp enchantment, and quite obviously, not enough warmth," said the old man as he fiddled with the lamp's wick. Then he tapped the oil-lamp twice on its side and immediately it began giving forth a warm and even flame. "Much better," muttered the old man as he sat down beside the young man and maiden," Much better indeed."

After they had sat and talked awhile, and the young man and maiden had caught the old man up on what every-one in the village was doing to ev-eryone else, the old man smiled and said, "Now that you have brought me the news, how is it that an old man may repay your kindness?" The young man looked at the maiden, and she looked back at him. Then, together they explained how they loved each other dearly but couldn't seem to get along together.

There was a long silence, during which the oil-lamp fell back to sputtering and the cold wind groaned in the igloo entrance, until finally the old man looked up at them and said, "This is a very difficult problem. There is no simple enchantment for something exactly like this, and I do not like to make up new ones because I am getting quite old, and, well, my spells these days often seem to leave something to be desired." At this the wind outside of the igloo seemed to groan especially loud, as if it were agreeing with him.

But the young man and maiden waited patiently, until the old man finally agreed to do what he could. He told them that they must not utter a single sound until he was through. Then he closed his eyes and began to sing a song.

He sang an enchantment song of wanting-someone-to-listen and added to it some want-attention rhyme, a few unselfish words and a good, solid live-happily-ever-after melody of which he was especially fond.

He sang on and on and on, and it seemed to the young man and maiden as if hours were passing. The old man's song soon began to sound to them like summer bees droning and they both fell fast asleep.

The young man immediately began to dream that he was lying in the snow, curled up warmly in a ball, a blue, cloudless arctic sky high above him. The snow had stopped falling and was sparkling everywhere and he felt as if everything about hem were exciting and new.

In fact, it was not that every-thing about him was different, but that he was differ-ent, for you see, he had become a sleek arctic wolf.

This was somewhat unsettling at first, but after a while, he became

more used to his new shape and senses, and began to take them for granted.

However, as the day wore on, and dusk came about him, he realized that he was all alone, and began to wonder what might have happened to the maiden.

Soon the night deepened about him, and he became very lonely. Around midnight or so, a strange feeling came over him as if someone were watching him and trying to catch his attention. He looked this way and that, but could see nothing out of the ordinary until at last he looked straight up, and there, brighter than the brightest

stars, and more beautiful than anything he had ever seen before, was a full arctic moon.

34

Its beauty and brightness immediately reminded him once again of the maiden, and before he knew what he was doing, he began to talk in wolf-sounds to the moon, telling it how lonely he was and how much he missed the maiden. There the moon remained, and seemed to listen intently to everything he said, shining even more brightly and beautifully.

After some time, the moon began to set behind the hills, and the wolf began to howl a sad promise-song. He promised that if ever he returned to his man-shape, and found the maiden, he would try his hardest to be unself-ish, to give her his attentions when she needed him, and to appreciate every mo-ment they might have together.

Now while all this was happening, the maiden dreamed a dream of her own in which she was high in the heavens, in the darkest of nights with millions of stars all about her, and she felt as if everything about her were exciting and new.

In fact, though, it was not that everything about her was different, but that she was different, for you see, she had become a full arctic moon.

This was unsettling at first, but after a short while, she came to like the halo of light which surrounded her, and the moonbeams which streamed from her touching everything she looked on with a pleasing radiance.

Still as the night wore on, she realized that she was alone, and began to wonder what had happened to the young man.

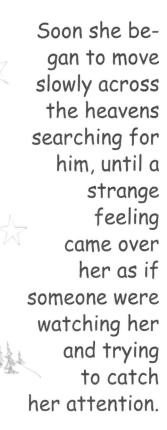

Soon she began to move slowly across the heavens searching for him, until a strange feeling came over her as if someone were watching her and trying to catch her attention.

She looked every which way, until at last she looked directly below her, and there, in the glow of her own moonlight she saw the most magnificent looking arctic wolf she had ever seen.

The wolf immediately reminded her of the young man she loved. Then, she noticed that the wolf was talking in wolf-sounds to her and, though she could not understand him, she realized that she understood his loneliness.

His song touched her heart, and she tried to shine brighter and more beautifully to let him know that she understood his loneliness and appreciated his attentions.

Finally, as she began to drift away, the wolf began to howl the saddest song she had ever heard, and she vowed that if ever she should return back to her maiden-self again, and found the young man she so dearly loved, she would try her best to be unselfish, to give him her attentions when he needed her, and to appreciate every mo-ment they might have together.

As the last note of the wolf's song echoed across the snow, the arctic moon reluctantly sank beneath the distant hills, and a great tiredness seemed to come over the wolf. He curled into a tight ball and fell into a deep sleep.

When the young man awoke, he was sitting back in the warm igloo, by the flickering oil-lamp, and the maiden was asleep with her head on his shoulder. She suddenly awakened, their eyes met and they saw each other in a way they had never been able to before.

Slowly they became aware of the old man sitting beside them, eyes still tightly closed, singing his strange song. The young man and maiden, not wanting to disturb the old man's singing, slipped into their parkas and mukluks and left quietly into the night.

So now, when winter is heaviest upon them, and the dark nights seem so cold that their igloo groans, the young man and maiden sit together before their own flickering seal oil-lamp, listening to the distant wolves sing to the arctic moon, and remember how happy they are for the moments they have together.

And the old man? When he realized that the young man and maiden had left before he could complete his enchantment, he took it and tossed it out into the winter night, and ever since, on cold, dark winter nights, there has been an aurora — what you probably call the northern lights.

Tale 3
Otter Girl

Once upon a time, not so very long ago really, there lived two sisters. Both were very beautiful and the treasures of their parents' hearts.

The first had long, black hair and black, liquid eyes. The other had dark brown hair and bright, sparkling eyes. Both had smiles that could melt even the hardest of men's hearts.

They were, however, also known for their practicality. So, when they both came to that age when a girl's fancies begins to turn to men, the first said, "Sister, it is time we began to find ourselves each a husband. I would like to find a handsome young man who can provide me with all the beautiful things which I am so fond of. The lawyer's son, who always looks so longingly at me, perhaps he should be the one for me. What about you, sister?"

"I will have only the prince of my dreams," said the second sister.

And so the days passed, and the two sisters pursued their interests. The first smiled back at the lawyer's son, accepting his favors and encouraging his advances, until one day he boldly asked her father for her hand in marriage and they were married in great splendor.

The second sister, how-
ever, stayed on with her
parents - that is, until they
began to ask her who was
she going to marry, and when
was she going to have
children like her sister.
In all kindness,
though sounding
rather stubborn
to them,
she told
her parents
firmly what she
had told her
sister: That she
would only marry the prince of her dreams.
Then she took kind leave of them and moved
into a small house at the edge of the village.

Every morning, before anyone in the village awakened, she would sit before her window alone, watching the sunrise and waiting for the prince of her dreams to come.

She spurned all suitors, and I must tell you, there were many: Some very wealthy, some very strong, and others very handsome. Day after day she

watched and waited, 'til some of the villagers began to say aloud, even when she was nearby, "There are no more princes. She will be unhappy and alone, and will finally die an old maid," and shook their heads slowly.

These were not kind words, and soon the girl began to despair. Still, she resolved to have none but the prince of her dreams.

One particularly fine morning, before any of the villagers even thought of stirring from their warm, cozy beds, she sat alone near her window, watching the sky lighten 'til only the Morning Star was left shining in the dawn sky. She closed her eyes tightly and made a special wish. And I'll tell you exactly what it was that she wished: She wished that the prince of her dreams would come. In fact, she made a solemn vow that if he did come, she would have him and no other.

As she completed her wish and opened her eyes, the Morning Star twinkled especially bright—and then suddenly faded as the first rays of sunshine streamed down from the sky, touching a spot below her window, flashing off something shiny.

She struggled forward to get a better look and to her surprise, there stood a handsome young man dressed in a fine fur coat. When she looked at him, he paused, tossed his head as if awakening, and looked up to her window. Their eyes met in wonder. This was indeed the prince of her dreams, standing just below her window, and she thought for a moment in her excitement how strange it was that she had not noticed him there just moments before!

52

But all such thoughts faded quickly under the gaze of his beautiful eyes. When at last he moved as if to call her, she put her finger to her lips to bid him be silent, and with a swish of her nightgown left the cabin and quietly descended the steps to meet him.

She stood before him, shyly, casting her eyes to the ground in fear that if she looked directly at him he might vanish into the thin morning air.

But he did not vanish and instead spoke to her in a strong, deep voice, "Dear maiden, you have come to me as if you knew me. Yet as I stand here before you, gazing on your beauty, I know that we have never met, for I could never forget someone as beautiful and radiant as you."

Slowly she lifted her gaze 'til at last their eyes met and she said to him, "Perhaps, but I have known you in my dreams for many years."

With that, he swept her into his arms and their lips met, he so tall and handsome in his furs, she resplendent in her nightgown, standing bare footed on tiptoes in the snow, and it seemed to her as if, indeed, they had been lovers for many years.

They talked in whispers for a while in each other's arms until at last he gently touched her cheek and said, "Beautiful maiden, your heart tells you right, for I am a prince in a great country far to the north. A long time ago, so long I can barely remember, I was enchanted by an old man and made to wander the earth, alone, 'til a maiden welcomed me back, though she had never known me, and would have no other 'til I return to her from the remainder of my wanderings, and then I will be free once again! But, if before I return, her heart should turn from me, for even an instant, the enchantment will change me forever into a lowly woodland creature."

The maiden said she understood all this, hugged and kissed her prince a final time, and then quickly tiptoed back up the stairs to her room. But when she looked down from her window to wish him just one more goodbye, the street was deserted and it was as if he had never been.

She looked and looked for him in vain, and eventually returned to her bed exhausted and fell fast asleep.

The next morning, when she awakened from her deep sleep—she was quite tired, you see, from the excitement of having met the prince of her dreams at last—she went to visit her parents and told them everything.

They were surprised, as you may well guess, and though it all seemed a bit strange to them, they assured her that they believed her story and would prepare for her wedding to the prince of her dreams, which they immediately began to make plans for.

But, as the days passed to weeks, and the weeks to months, her parents began once again to say to her, "Dearest daughter, there really are no such princes. They only exist in our dreams."

Soon the villagers began to say once again when they were near her, "There are no more princes. Unless she gives up this folly, she will remain alone, unhappy and die an old maid."

At first she ignored their idle talk and faithfully kept her morning vigil. But as the months wore on, her parents, the villagers, and even people she didn't know, began saying right to her face, "You know, there really, truly are no more princes. Her prince was a dream of her lonely heart. She will be alone and will die an old maid," and the girl began to despair.

Even her best girl friends said to her, "There are no more princes," and begged her to her to go out for just one evening with any one of the willing young men of the village. And though she refused kindly, and continued her morning vigil, she began to find herself worrying for her prince's safety.

At last she could stand it no longer and began to wonder, "Could it have been just a dream after all?"

Finally, at her parent's pleading—and canny suggestion—she finally consented to go for a walk the next morning to a nearby field, and bring breakfast to a neighboring hunter's son, who had continued to love her dearly all these months and had never given her up, no matter how silly she was about dreams and princes and other such nonsense.

Very early next morning, just before dawn, she set off with her basket to meet the hunter's son. She walked and walked, humming a particularly happy tune, until at last she came to a small, sparkling stream, and there paused to admire the dawn.

When only the Morning Star was left shining in the lightening sky, it suddenly twinkled especially bright and began to fade as the first rays of sunshine peeked above the horizon, touching a spot on the bank of the stream not far from where she stood, and flashed off something shiny.

When she blinked her eyes, there before her once again stood the prince of her dreams, wrapped in his furs. He paused, shook his head as if awakening, looked up at her, and the moment their eyes met, reached out his arms. As she reached for him, her eyes beaming with all the love she had stored in her heart for him, she suddenly remembered her promise which she had only just this moment broken, and a tear began to fall from her eyes.

The prince looked into her eyes, first with puzzlement and then with sadness as the tear grew, until another ray of morning sunshine flashed as it touched her tear. She blinked her eyes, and when she opened them, the prince of her dreams was gone and in his place stood a small, brown otter with sad, brown eyes.

The maiden dropped her basket and ran to the otter, who was already turning to slide down the bank and into the stream, and cried, "Once I had a dream and a wish. Now it is gone forever. I wish that I had never wished, for now I am so unhappy I will surely die."

Just then, the first gust of morning wind swept by her, took up her cries and carried them up to where winter itself begins in the farthest north. There an old man lived, who had long ago cast a spell on an innocent prince and very greatly regretted his wrong.

He heard the maiden's cries of anguish and they cut deeply into his
heart. Even so, he knew that so powerful an enchantment, once done,
cannot be undone and so he could only
add his cry of sorrow to hers.

Now, as fate would have it, their
cries together reached all the way
to the highest heavens, and together
shattered the Book of Enchantments
where promises once made are forever recorded, and instantly, the
maiden turned into an otter.

And so, dear reader, to this very day,
otters are happy and
joyful creatures,
for they know
the importance
of dreams and
wishes, and
how good
it is to
finally be
together
with some-
one you love,
no matter
what the
circumstances.

But their story
didn't end there,
because you see,
nowadays, enchantments
and promises are allowed to be written
only in the hearts of humans
instead of the book of heaven.